Harriet
the
Beach Cat

by Leah Hudson

Dedications

To Sharon Hewing, founder of the Skiathos Cat Welfare Association,
for her kind and generous heart and many years of devotion.

To the SCWA volunteers worldwide
for being of service to the voiceless.

To Philip Bloom for shining a light on Sharon, the SCWA,
and the plight of stray cats in Skiathos.

To Eleanor and Paul for inspiring hearts to change.

ISBN: 9781098963644

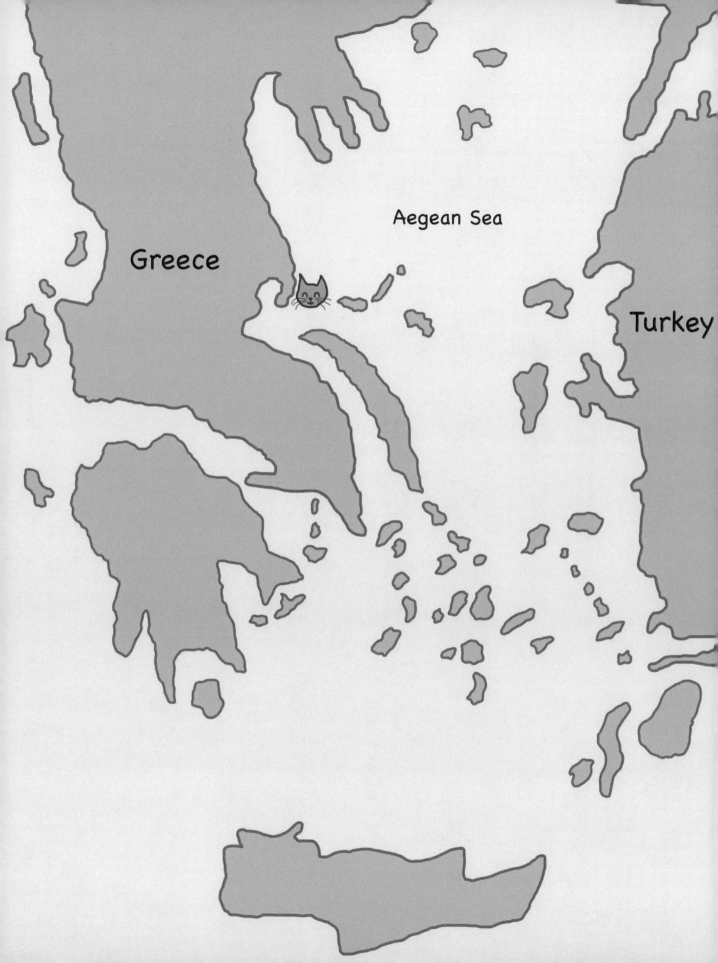

Greece

Aegean Sea

Turkey

For Harriet

It's summertime on the tiny island of Skiathos. The town is bustling and a delicious, smoky haze hangs in the air, mingling with a salty sea breeze.

Warm weather means more tourists, and dozens of stray cats work their way from one end of town to the other, craving both attention and handouts.

Harriet cautiously weaves her way past hotels and pubs glancing up shyly, every so often, in search of friendly faces in the crowd. Her right eye has recently been stitched up, and she worries that some of the tourists—especially the smaller ones—might be a bit frightened by her appearance.

Even without her injury, Harriet knows that it's best to be wary. She has heard many unfortunate tales of cats who've been a little too trusting. However, a life filled with uncertainties is very unsettling, and Harriet dreams of having a home of her own someday.

Like most of the stray cats on the island, she has grown quite accustomed to life on the streets and beaches of Skiathos, and considers herself fairly independent. But that's because she's had to be for as long as she can remember.

With a full tummy Harriet makes her way down to the beach, hoping to find a safe place to take a nap. Navigating the island gets much trickier this time of year because more visitors means more cars…and more cars means crossing busier streets. Harriet has seen for herself what can happen to a cat who darts into traffic without looking both ways first.

At the top of the beach parking lot on a shady, grass-covered hill Harriet sits for a moment to survey the beach before continuing down to the cool, soft sand. Her friend, Severus, is sunbathing on a lounge chair near a large group of tourists, and not too far away is a man sitting by himself on a blue blanket.

He looks up at her as she casually strolls past him, and she searches his face to be sure it's safe to approach. The man has a warm, friendly smile and he pats a spot next to him on the blanket.

Harriet gratefully accepts belly rubs, chin scratches, and long, head to toe strokes of her fur. It's a relief to be able to relax for a while, and it's moments like this that make Harriet long for the comfort and security of a place to call home.

The man unzips his bag and offers Harriet a few savory cat treats. If she'd known before her breakfast of table scraps in town, she would've much preferred his offering. Her tummy aches a little, but Harriet doesn't want to seem impolite, so she graciously accepts the morsels but nibbles them slowly.

The man takes pictures of her, and also of the beach and the boats on the big water.

After wiping her face, Harriet settles in close to the man and falls asleep. She feels warm and cozy, inside and out.

By the time Harriet wakes up, the sun is low in the sky and the man is gathering his belongings. He seems reluctant to leave, however, and lingers for a while as other beach goers make their way to the parking lot.

The man opens his bag again, this time to take pictures of an orange and yellow sky as the sun melts into the water. When he turns around to take a few more of Harriet, she sits up tall and adjusts herself ever so slightly to hide her prickly looking stitches.

Harriet follows the man to his car. He speaks to her softly before starting the engine and slowly driving away.

Every day Harriet returns to the same spot at the same beach to spend time with her new companion. And as she drifts off to sleep with a full tummy, she dreams of what life might be like if he took her home with him.

She imagines what it would be like to live without the usual daily worries of busy streets, unfavorable weather, and unpredictable encounters with people and other animals.

Harriet wakes up and quickly bathes so she can get down to the beach early and wait for the man with the blue blanket. There's a nip in the air but Harriet doesn't give it a second thought. She will be perfectly comfortable curled up next to the man at the beach.

But as she makes her way through town, which is the quickest way to the beach, Harriet can't help but notice something else. Several restaurants have closed their doors, hung signs in their windows, and stacked chairs tightly against buildings. The vibrant rhythm of music and chatter has become dim and distant, now that the summer crowds have dwindled.

Harriet suddenly realizes that there have already been many sleeps of wonderful warm weather, and now the long season of wind and rain grows near. She can't wait to see her new friend and spend the day snuggled up next to him on the big blue blanket.

When she arrives at the grassy hill, though, Harriet sees more signs of change. Lounge chairs have been stacked and umbrellas closed and tied shut. No one is swimming and the breeze feels much stronger than it did in town.

The man who sells boat rides is gone, and all of his boats have been overturned and placed on a rack.

Severus peers cautiously from beneath one of the upside-down boats and for a moment Harriet considers joining him, but then quickly remembers why she's come here in the first place.

The man with the blue blanket is nowhere to be seen. Harriet looks up and down the beach, squinting her good eye to see if she recognizes any of the people walking along the shore. Perhaps he just hasn't arrived yet? Or maybe he's taking pictures further down the beach?

For a long time she waits, until the wind begins to blow even harder and specks of rain dot her face and fur.

Soon sprinkles become large drips, and Harriet takes cover beneath a tower of chairs. There is probably a more comfortable spot, where the wind wouldn't ruffle her coat, but Harriet doesn't want to lose sight of the place where the man with the blue blanket sits.

She knows that many cold sleeps are coming now. Soon people and food will be scarce, and Harriet starts to feel lonely. She shivers as a tear trickles off the tip of her nose.

It's wintertime now. Most of the shops in Skiathos have locked their doors and shuttered their windows.

Harriet makes her way to a feeding station just outside of town near a wooded park. A kind woman comes every day to leave food and water for the stray cats on the island and Harriet looks forward to seeing her. The man has been gone for many sleeps, but Harriet still visits the beach every day to look for him.

To help keep her mind off the cold, Harriet takes a different route today, and as she skirts the outer edge of town she sees two scruffy-looking kittens rummaging through the contents of an overturned garbage can. They look up as Harriet approaches, hissing at her and guarding their treasure.

But the closer she gets, the more frightened they seem and Harriet feels sorry for them. Surely there will be plenty of kibble to go around at the park, so she encourages them to join her. Much to her surprise the dirty, hungry orphans obediently follow.

Harriet feels a bit like a mama cat and wonders how long the kittens have been wandering around alone. There are many more like them on the island, but she's never seen these two before.

They arrive at the feeding station a bit early and the kittens look worried as a light rain begins to fall. They gather beneath a thick cluster of trees to stay dry, and the kittens sit quite close to her. They seem to trust Harriet, who appreciates their company and the warmth of huddling together.

Soon she hears the familiar sound of the woman's car. Harriet's tummy grumbles, but she waits patiently with the kittens until food has been poured and water bowls are filled.

The woman gasps when the three of them emerge from their shelter and as soon as the kittens finish eating she picks them up and inspects them carefully, one at a time.

"Buhbuhbuh-BUP!"

The woman nuzzles their filthy little faces, and then turns her attention to Harriet. She seems genuinely happy to see her, and always makes Harriet feel loved. Her voice is as gentle and comforting as her touch, and for a moment Harriet wishes it was still summer. She misses the man with the blue blanket and warm smile. He makes her feel this way too.

More sleeps pass, and Harriet spends most of her days in search of food and safe places to rest. At night, she usually sleeps on the covered porch of an elderly woman who doesn't leave her house much, but occasionally treats Harriet to a can of tuna or leftover bits of chicken. She never shoos Harriet away, but her dog barks incessantly at Harriet whenever it sees her so she usually leaves as early as possible to avoid being noticed.

Sometimes she sleeps with Severus at the beach, but if he happens to find somewhere more pleasant it's much too chilly without him, and also a bit unsettling to be so far away from houses and people.

As the sun disappears and countless twinkling lights awaken in the sky, Harriet strolls past mostly empty shops in town and heads for the old woman's porch.

Suddenly, from somewhere in the darkness ahead she hears a tiny sound. It's so faint that for a moment Harriet wonders if she has imagined it.

"Meooooowww…"

Harriet sniffs the crisp night air and quickens her step.

"Meooooowww…"

A cardboard box sits on the curb in front of a pink house, next to some garbage cans. Harriet cautiously peers inside and immediately recognizes her friend, Gingernuts! He's clearly been injured and is in a great deal of pain.

"Meooooowww…" His cry is quiet and sad.

Harriet knows that it could be dangerous to stay, but cannot imagine leaving her friend alone. She also doesn't want him to give up hope. Perhaps a kind-hearted person will find him in the morning, and take him to the vet, just like the woman from the park had done for her when she was found in the dumpster downtown.

Harriet carefully climbs into the box next to Gingernuts, gently licking the nick on his ear, and snuggling in tightly to comfort him and keep him warm. He makes no sound, and soon they both fall asleep.

Harriet wakes up to the low rumble of a garbage truck lumbering up the street. Gingernuts lay motionless, his breathing still slow and steady. Harriet cannot move him all by herself, so she hides in some nearby bushes and hopes that the garbage truck driver is as caring as the woman at the park and the man with the blue blanket.

Harriet anxiously waits, her heart thumping like a drum in her chest as the truck pulls up to the pink house, and a man hops out from the other side.

He kneels beside the box, and Harriet studies his expression as he gingerly reaches inside to examine and reassure Gingernuts. His voice is low and soothing as he carefully picks up the box and straps it into the passenger side of the garbage truck.

Harriet feels confident that her friend is safe, and hopes that one day he, too, might find a forever home.

It has been a long and lonely winter. As the weather slowly begins to change, Harriet notices a familiar feeling of excitement in town. She's hoping for a quick bite to eat before heading to her favorite beach.

But instead of quieting her hungry tummy, Harriet somehow finds herself face to face with a very large and very angry-looking dog.

No leash, no collar, and as it lunges at her Harriet manages to escape by climbing up the nearest tree and clutching the highest branch she can reach.

Harriet struggles for a moment to catch her breath, swallowing hard to fight back a well of tears that make the town and people below a colorful blur.

When the dog finally loses interest in her, a very shaken and extra cautious Harriet hurries on her way.

Pausing at her favorite lookout, Harriet takes a deep breath of sea air. Here, too, are signs of warmer weather ahead. Lounge chairs are neatly lined up, with an open umbrella between each pair. The man who sells boat rides is turning boats right side up and wiping them off with towels. People are strolling up and down the shoreline, squealing every time the foamy water splashes their ankles.

At first Harriet is so distracted that she doesn't even notice the blue blanket, or the man sitting with his bags and his camera.

Can it be?

Without looking away, Harriet hurries toward the man. The moment he catches sight of her a smile fills his face. His eyes sparkle like flecks of sunlight flickering on the water, and as soon as Harriet gets close enough he cradles her in his arms and kisses her cheek. He pours kibble into a bowl and offers water from the lid of his canteen. She devours the tasty breakfast and stays with the man all day. Harriet cannot believe her luck, and wonders how many sleeps they will have together before he leaves again.

But as the sun dips into the big water, and he begins to gather his belongings, Harriet observes something different about the man's face as he packs up his car and drives away. It tugs at her heart as she walks back to town and the old woman's porch.

After a restless night, Harriet is more excited than ever to get to the beach. She quickly makes her way past the sights and sounds of visitors in town, and arrives so early that the grassy hill is still wet with dew.

Severus is fast asleep near the boats, and the man who sells boat rides hasn't arrived yet. People are scattered here and there, collecting shells, tossing rocks into the water, and making lines in the wet sand with sticks of driftwood.

Her tummy grumbles, and for a moment Harriet considers going back to town for breakfast. But as she turns to leave a car pulls up quite close to her.

The man with the blue blanket steps out and greets Harriet warmly, as usual, but he isn't dressed for a day at the beach and he doesn't unload the car. He does, however, pour food and water for her, waiting patiently for Harriet to finish eating and cleaning her face before scooping her up and gently placing her in a kennel.

Harriet is confused, but unafraid, and after a short drive he stops the car and takes her out again. She is immediately surrounded by a large group of cats that seem very curious and excited to greet her.

A smiling woman appears and Harriet recognizes her in an instant.

"Buhbuhbuh-BUP!"

It's the woman from the park! She coos at Harriet, kissing her repeatedly on the top of her head, and also on the spot where her eye used to be.

It has been many sleeps, and her memory is a bit foggy, but Harriet soon realizes that she has been here before. This is where she'd been taken to recover after her accident.

Harriet enjoys getting reacquainted with old friends at the woman's home. Every day the man comes to see her and the other cats. He brings treats, takes pictures, and plays with them for hours.

During her stay at the woman's home, Harriet gets a checkup from the same veterinarian who'd tended to her wounds and stitched up her right eye. He is very gentle, and by the sound of his voice and the smile on his face Harriet can tell he is pleased to see how well she has healed.

Cats swirl around the woman's ankles as she hugs the man and tells them both goodbye.

"Buhbuhbuh-BUP!"

She presses her lips to Harriet's cheek once more, and again, Harriet is placed in a kennel in the man's car.

But before she has time to wonder about their next destination, Harriet suddenly feels quite drowsy, so she makes herself comfortable and quickly falls asleep.

When she wakes, Harriet feels as though many sleeps have passed. She's very thirsty, and the air smells different.

It doesn't smell like the town, or the beach, or the porch, or the park. It also doesn't smell like the man's car, or the vet, or the shed at the woman's house.

Harriet stands up to stretch on trembling legs, and discovers that she's been removed from the kennel and tucked into a fuzzy blanket.

Bewildered and excited, she looks around the room filled with strange furnishings, wanting to explore her new surroundings but still feeling a bit woozy and wondering if it's all just a dream.

Harriet's tummy grumbles and suddenly she feels quite alone.

"Meooow," she calls out, curiously.

A door opens, and the man from the beach appears, smiling as usual.

"This is where you live now, Harriet," he says, carrying her from room to room and introducing her to four other cats.

"And this is your new family."

Harriet can hardly believe her ears. A brand new feeling washes over her like a wave smoothing out the sand.

No more relying on strangers for food or rummaging through smelly garbage cans. No more sleeping on drafty porches or wet beaches. No more dodging cars or running from dogs or hiding in trees. Never again feeling scared or lonely.

Harriet's dreams have finally come true.

"Welcome home, Harriet," the man says.

"Welcome home."

About the Author

Leah Hudson lives in Northern California with her husband, kids, chickens and bunny. She was inspired to start writing children's books about the cats of Skiathos after watching documentary films about them by award-winning British filmmaker Philip Bloom. Leah's first book, *Miss Sharon and the Cats of Skiathos*, is available worldwide on Amazon. Visit Leah on Instagram **@leah.hudson.writes**

About the Illustrator

12 year old daughter of the author, Ava Hudson loves animals—especially cats. She began a personal fundraising effort to help support the SCWA after watching Mr. Bloom's videos.

Proceeds from this book are donated to the
Skiathos Cat Welfare Association
(Greek Registered Charity No: 2177/2011)

Since 2005 Sharon Hewing has been caring for the cats of Skiathos, and in 2007 she formed the Skiathos Cat Welfare Association (SCWA). Run entirely by volunteers and donations, her organization has fed, neutered, medicated, rehabilitated, and cared for thousands of homeless cats on the island. To learn more, visit **skiathos-cats.org**

Philip Bloom is an award-winning filmmaker, cat lover, and friend of the SCWA. To see the films that inspired this story, go to **bit.ly/theskiathoscats** or scan the QR code below. To keep up with Harriet and her family, follow them on Instagram **@thebloomcats**

Made in the USA
Middletown, DE
24 June 2023